BETSY and
MR. KILPATRICK

By the Same Author

BETSY and
MR. KILPATRICK

written and
illustrated by
CAROLYN
HAYWOOD

William Morrow and Company
New York

JF
H

Fourth Printing, December 1970

885

To

Barbara Brighten,

this book is lovingly dedicated.

CONTENTS

BETSY and
MR. KILPATRICK

Chapter 1

MR. KILPATRICK

MR. KILPATRICK was the policeman who saw the children across the big, wide street. Every school day he parked his red car near the corner where the children crossed on their way to school. There were always busses and trucks and cars passing, and the children waited for Mr. Kilpatrick to hold up the traffic while they crossed to the other side.

All of the children looked upon Mr. Kilpatrick as their friend. He was a big man with a deep chuckly voice and a twinkle in his blue eyes. Before the children were through the first grade he knew all of their names. Mr. Kilpatrick was Irish, and he joked with the children in his warm Irish voice as they went back and forth across the street. "Good morning, Little Red Ribbons!" he would say, when he saw Betsy. "That's a fine new hairdo you've got." Then, looking at Betsy's little sister Star, he would say, "And how is little Twinkle this morning?" Mr. Kilpatrick's greetings rolled over and over on his tongue.

Betsy said to her friend, Billy Porter, one morning, "You know, when Mr. Kilpatrick says good morning, the words sound like happy thunder."

"That's right!" Billy replied. "They do. And Mr. Kilpatrick is strong too. I bet if anybody tried to do anything wrong, Mr. Kilpatrick would go after him like a ball of lightning."

"That's right," Betsy agreed. "Just like a ball of lightning."

Mr. Kilpatrick not only saw the children across the street, he also appeared, as if by magic, as soon as any child was in trouble. Mr. Kilpatrick was always rescuing somebody. Cats and dogs and birds, as well as children. The children were always glad to see his bright red car drive through their streets. Mr. Kilpatrick was indeed the children's friend.

There was also Mrs. Kilpatrick, a round, warm, bouncy woman, who Betsy said reminded her of a picture of Mrs. Do-as-you-would-be-done-by in her copy of Kingsley's *Water Babies*. Although Mrs. Kilpatrick did not appear as miraculously as Mr. Kilpatrick when help was needed, many of the children knew her because the Kilpatricks lived near the school. Children who knew both Mr. and Mrs. Kilpatrick felt twice blessed.

One afternoon Betsy and Ellen were standing by the fence in front of Betsy's house, when Mr. Kilpatrick passed in his car. The girls waved to him and he waved back. When he had passed out of sight, Betsy said, "It's sad, isn't it, that Mr. and Mrs. Kilpatrick haven't any boys or girls of their own?"

"I don't know!" Ellen replied. "I never thought of it. Maybe they don't want any."

"I'm sure they would love to have some children of their own," said Betsy. "At least one. Look how nice they are to all of us."

"If they had children of their own, they might not have time to be so nice to us," said Ellen.

"That's selfish, Ellen!" said Betsy. "It's selfish not to want Mr. and Mrs. Kilpatrick to have any children of their own."

"I didn't say I didn't want them to have any,"

said Ellen. "They can have all they want. They can have a hundred children if they want. I don't care."

"Oh, nobody wants a hundred children!" exclaimed Betsy. "That's silly! What makes you think they would want a hundred children?"

"I didn't say I thought they wanted a hundred children," Ellen replied. "I said they could have a hundred children if they wanted them."

Just then Billy Porter wheeled up on his bicycle and stopped by Betsy's gate. "Hi!" he called out. "Who's got a hundred children?"

"Oh, nobody you know," said Betsy. "We're having a private conversation."

"Is that so!" said Billy. "Well, nobody in the whole world could have a hundred children."

"Rabbits could," said Ellen, as Billy wheeled around in a circle.

"We're not talking about rabbits, Ellen," said Betsy. "We're talking about Mr. and Mrs. Kilpatrick." As soon as Billy heard the word *rabbits,* he exclaimed, "You mean Mr. and Mrs. Kilpatrick have rabbits? I'm going right over there and see them. I love rabbits! Maybe they will give me one." Without waiting a moment, Billy started off on his bicycle.

"Oh, dear!" said Betsy. "Now Billy is going over to the Kilpatricks to get a rabbit, and the Kilpatricks don't have rabbits."

"How do you know they don't have rabbits?" said Ellen. "Loads of people have rabbits."

"I don't know one single person who has rabbits," said Betsy, "and I don't know why we're talking about rabbits anyway."

"You said Mr. and Mrs. Kilpatrick didn't have any children," said Ellen, "and I said that rabbits did."

"Did what?" Betsy asked.

"Have children," Ellen replied.

"Rabbits do not have children, Ellen," said Betsy. "They have rabbits."

"Well, aren't rabbits' rabbits, rabbits' children?" Ellen asked.

"I guess rabbits' rabbits are rabbits' children," said Betsy, "but I don't see what rabbits have to do with Mr. and Mrs. Kilpatrick."

"Just that Billy has gone to see if the Kilpatricks have any rabbits," Ellen answered, "and I think we should go over and see, too. Maybe they do have rabbits."

"All right," Betsy replied, "let's go." The girls ran to their bicycles that were leaning against the fence. Then they mounted them and rode off. As they turned into the street where Mr. and Mrs. Kilpatrick lived, Betsy and Ellen could see Billy and Mrs. Kilpatrick in the front yard.

When the girls rode up, Billy called out, "Here they are now!"

"Hi, Billy!" Betsy shouted. "Hello, Mrs. Kilpatrick!"

"Well, if it isn't Betsy!" said Mrs. Kilpatrick,

with her bright smile. "I was asking Mr. Kilpatrick about you only yesterday. It's been a long time since you last dropped by." Then she said, "And Ellen, here! It's good to see you."

"It's always nice to see you, Mrs. Kilpatrick," Ellen replied.

The girls parked their bicycles by the white picket fence and joined Billy. He said, "Say, Betsy! Mrs. Kilpatrick doesn't have any rabbits."

Mrs. Kilpatrick laughed. "Whatever made you think we had rabbits, Betsy?" she asked.

"I didn't," said Betsy. "It was Ellen. I wasn't talking about rabbits. I wasn't even thinking about rabbits. I was just talking about children."

Mrs. Kilpatrick laughed again. "Well, we haven't any children either," she said. "All we have are you boys and girls at the school, and a fine bunch you are most of the time. Pat was talking the other night. 'Sure, Mary!' he said to me. 'They're little divils at times, but I never met one yet I couldn't love. I just set my mind to it.' "

"Mr. Kilpatrick is a swell policeman," said Billy. "He's the best ever!"

"Yes," Betsy agreed. "He's our friend!"

"I don't know what we'd do without him," said Ellen.

"We've known him ever since we were in the first grade," said Betsy.

"Now we're in the fourth," said Billy.

"You're getting big," said Mrs. Kilpatrick.

After the children had talked for a while they got ready to leave. Mrs. Kilpatrick said, "I'm sorry I haven't got a rabbit for you, Billy."

"That's O.K.," Billy called back.

"Good-bye!" the children shouted to Mrs. Kilpatrick, riding off down the street.

Mrs. Kilpatrick waved to the children. She watched them until they were out of sight. As she turned to go back into the house, she said aloud to herself, "Sure, it will be a shock to them. I do hope they won't take it too hard."

Chapter 2

THE CHILDREN HEAR
THE NEWS

SEVERAL MORNINGS later, when she reached
the school yard, Betsy found a group of children crowded around Eddie Wilson. She el-
bowed her way between the children and heard
Eddie say, "It is so true!"

"I don't believe it," Ellen said. "You're making it all up."

Betsy saw that all of the children were looking very solemn.

"It's true, I tell you!" said Eddie.

"What is it? What is it?" said Betsy.

"Eddie says that Mr. Kilpatrick is going to be removed," Ellen replied.

"Removed!" Betsy repeated. "What do you mean, *removed*?"

"He isn't going to see us across the street anymore," said Ellen. "A lady is going to be at the crossing."

"A lady!" cried Betsy. "What kind of a lady?"

"A police lady, I guess," Billy piped up.

"I don't believe it's true," said Betsy. "I won't believe it unless Mr. Kilpatrick tells me, and I'm going right back to ask him."

Betsy turned to run out of the yard, but at that moment the school bell rang and the children had to go into their classrooms. As Betsy followed Ellen, she said, "You don't think it's true about Mr. Kilpatrick, do you, Ellen?"

"Oh, you know Eddie Wilson!" Ellen replied. "He's always bursting with some news. He loves to give out information."

When the children reached their classroom, Betsy said to her teacher, "Miss Richards, it isn't true that Mr. Kilpatrick is going to be removed, is it?"

Billy said, "Say it isn't true, Miss Richards."

"Yes," cried several children. "Say it isn't true."

Miss Richards looked at the troubled faces, and said, "I'm afraid it is true. I'm sorry I have to tell you. You see Mr. Kilpatrick is being promoted, so we should all be glad for him."

The whole class stood silent, looking at Miss Richards. "But—but," said Betsy at last, "what will we do without Mr. Kilpatrick?"

"Are we really going to get a lady in place of Mr. Kilpatrick?" Kenny Roberts asked.

"Yes, I believe so," Miss Richards replied.

Billy threw himself into his seat and put his head between his hands. "Oh, no!" he cried. "A lady! A lady policeman!"

"Now what is wrong with a lady policeman?" their teacher asked.

"It's awful!" cried several of the children together.

"You have a lady teacher," said Miss Richards. "You don't think that is awful. Why not a lady policeman?"

"Because!" was the chorus that came forth from the children.

"Because we love Mr. Kilpatrick!" said Betsy. "And Mr. Kilpatrick loves us."

"Well, the change won't take place for quite some time," said Miss Richards. "Mr. Kilpatrick will be with us until the first of November."

"It's the middle of September now," said Ellen.

"Maybe the police chief won't find any lady who wants to be a policeman," said Kenny.

Just then the bell rang for school to begin, and Miss Richards said, "We won't talk about Mr. Kilpatrick anymore today. It's time to have our arithmetic."

At noon, in the lunchroom, Eddie Wilson, who was not in Betsy's class, stopped at her table. "Well!" he said. "Was I right about Mr. Kilpatrick?"

"Oh, yes!" Betsy sighed. "You were right. But you sound as though you didn't care."

"Of course, I care!" said Eddie. "Mr. Kilpatrick's my friend just as much as he is yours."

Betsy could hardly wait to see Mr. Kilpatrick on her way home that afternoon. When school was out, she quickly found Star and hurried to the corner where Mr. Kilpatrick was standing. He was already surrounded by children. "Mr. Kilpatrick!" Betsy called. "You can't leave us! You can't! What will we do without you?"

"What will we do?" Star echoed.

"You'll get along all right," Mr. Kilpatrick

replied. "You'll have a nice lady to take care of you. There's no cause for you to fret. The trouble is what am I going to do without all of you children? Lonesome I'll be without you."

"We'll miss you, Mr. Kilpatrick," the children chorused. "We'll miss you."

"No lady policeman will be as nice as you," said Ellen, who had just joined the group.

Mr. Kilpatrick laughed. "Now, Ellen," he said, "get along with your sweet talk. In Ireland they'd say that you kissed the Blarney stone."

"What's the Blarney stone?" Ellen asked.

"Yes, Mr. Kilpatrick, tell us about the Blarney stone," said Betsy.

"And do you think I'm here to tell you stories?" said Mr. Kilpatrick. "I'm here to hold up the traffic and see that you all get over to the other side of the street."

"But we don't want to go over to the other side of the street," said Ellen. "We want to hear about the Blarney stone."

Mr. Kilpatrick looked down at the group of children around him. More children had joined the crowd. "Mr. Kilpatrick is going to tell us about the Blarney stone," said Betsy.

For several minutes everyone forgot about the cars and trucks going by. Drivers as they passed looked at the policeman surrounded by the many children. "I'll bet he's giving them a piece of his mind," said a woman sitting beside her husband in one of the cars.

"Must be a hard job to hold those kids down," her husband replied. "I bet he's tough with them."

"Well! It's like this," Mr. Kilpatrick was saying. "In Ireland, where I come from, there's a castle, called Blarney castle. It's near Cork."

"I know what a cork is," Star piped up. "You pull it out of a bottle."

"This Cork is a city," said Mr. Kilpatrick, "and Blarney castle is near Cork."

"And does a princess live in the castle?" asked Betsy.

"No, there's no princess in it," said Mr. Kilpatrick. "This isn't a fairy tale and don't interrupt. I have to tell it fast. Just look at how many children are waiting to go home."

"We don't want to go across, Mr. Kilpatrick," said Ellen. "We just want to hear about the Blarney stone."

"Well, there's this castle," said Mr. Kilpatrick.

"Blarney castle," said Star.

"Near Cork," said Ellen.

"Right!" said Mr. Kilpatrick. "And up near the top of one of the towers, there's a stone."

"Is it a little stone or a big stone?" one of the children asked.

"It's a pretty big stone," said Mr. Kilpatrick.

"Could I lift it?" asked Billy.

"No, you couldn't lift it, Billy. Moreover, it's

fastened into the wall," said Mr. Kilpatrick. "Just look at all you children."

"Go on, Mr. Kilpatrick," said Betsy.

"Well, the story is that anyone who kisses this stone, will be saying sweet talk all his life and making everybody feel pleased with himself."

"How can anyone kiss the stone if it's up at the top of a tower?" asked Billy. "Is there a ladder?"

"Not exactly," replied Mr. Kilpatrick. "There are winding stairs. Just look at all you children. A person has to climb up to the top and lie down on his back. Then his head is hanging out. The Blarney stone is right above him, and he can give it a big kiss."

"How does he keep from falling out?" cried Billy.

"How many people have fallen out?" asked Eddie Wilson.

"Nobody falls out, because someone is there to hold on to everyone's feet," Mr. Kilpatrick replied. "Now come along, the whole bunch of you. Over to the other side." Mr. Kilpatrick blew his whistle at last. The cars stopped and the crowd of children followed Mr. Kilpatrick.

On the way, Betsy said, "Oh, Mr. Kilpatrick, I don't think the lady policeman will tell us the nice stories that you can tell."

"Now just remember, she's not coming to tell you stories. She's coming to see that you get across the street safely. Directing traffic is a safety job, not a storytelling job."

"But you do both, Mr. Kilpatrick," said Betsy. "You're wonderful."

"Sure, Little Red Ribbons, a fairy must have touched your tongue with dust from the Blarney stone," said Mr. Kilpatrick.

Chapter 3

THE KILPATRICK CLUB

THE FOLLOWING day Betsy and Ellen were
sitting beside each other at a table in the
cafeteria. Betsy had just put down a bowl of
tomato soup and Ellen had just opened up a
peanut-butter sandwich, when Billy Porter

joined them. He had a bowl of pea soup. As he put it on the table, he said, "Looks like green paint, doesn't it?"

"You wouldn't eat it if it was," said Kenny, sitting down beside Billy. Kenny opened up a currant-jelly sandwich.

Then Mary Lou came and joined the group. She was carrying a plate of egg salad.

Soon all of the places at the table were filled. Betsy looked at the children around her while she stirred her soup in order to cool it. Betsy had known all of them ever since she had been in the first grade. There was Peter eating a piece of blueberry pie and Christopher munching on a minced-ham sandwich. There were the Taylor twins, Richard and Henry. Richard was eating a large piece of gingerbread, while Henry ate a cupcake covered with thick chocolate icing along with his soup. There was Betty Jane with a cheese sandwich in one hand and a large pickle in the other.

Betsy went on stirring her soup. In a few moments she said, "I've been thinking about Mr. Kilpatrick."

"What about him?" Ellen asked.

"Well, I was just thinking. Everybody at this table is a special friend of Mr. Kilpatrick. Right?"

All the children around the table called out, "Yes!"

"And we're all sorry Mr. Kilpatrick is leaving us. Right?"

"Right!" the children chorused.

"Then I think this table should be for Mr. Kilpatrick's special friends," said Betsy.

"I think so too," said Ellen.

"So," said Betsy. "Let's make it a club. The Kilpatrick Club."

"Yes!" everyone agreed.

"I'll be the president," said Billy.

"No!" exclaimed Ellen. "We have to vote for a president."

"Well, let's vote now," said Kenny, taking a bite of his currant-jelly sandwich. Some of the currant jelly dropped out.

"We haven't any paper to write the names on," said Betsy. "We have to write the name of the person we vote for."

"I'll get a clean paper napkin," said Billy, leaving his chair. Billy went to the lunch counter and asked for another napkin. When he came back to the table, he said, "I'll divide it up."

"We need nine pieces," said Betsy. "One for each of us."

"I can't tear it into nine," said Billy. "I can only fold this napkin into eight even pieces, and the pieces have to be even so no one knows how we vote."

"Yes," said Betsy. "That's very important. The voting has to be secret."

Billy looked at the napkin in his hand, and said, "I can't fold it into nine pieces. I can only make eight." His forehead was wrinkled up.

"Well, come on Bill," said Peter. "The bell will ring before we have time to vote."

"O.K.!" said Billy. "I won't vote. I think I'm going to be elected president anyway."

"Don't be too sure," said Henry. Billy set to work, first folding the napkin in half and tearing it along the crease. Then he folded each half and tore each piece in two. "Now that's four," he said. He folded one of the four pieces and tore it across the middle.

"That's five," said Ellen.

Billy folded and tore another piece.

"That makes six," said Christopher.

Billy tore the two remaining pieces of paper. "Now you have eight," said Betsy.

Billy handed a ballot to each of the children around the table. Everyone wrote something on his paper, shielding it with his hands so that no one could see what he was writing.

"I'll count the votes," said Betsy, "because I was the one who thought of the club." No one objected to Betsy counting the votes, so she got up and walked around the table collecting the papers. Each slip was folded several times so that no one could see what was written on it.

After Betsy had collected all of the ballots she began to open them. "Call 'em out, Betsy," said Billy. "I'll write 'em down."

"All right," said Betsy, opening the first one. It had a bit of egg on it. She read out, "One vote for Mary Lou." Then she picked up the second one. It was stuck together with something that looked like blueberry pie. "One for Peter," she said. The third one had a greasy smudge of minced ham on it. "One for Christopher," said Betsy. The next one smelled strongly of vinegar, as though it had been near a pungent pickle. "One for Betty Jane," she said.

Betsy thought some of the papers were very messy as she picked up another ballot. "Oh!" she said, opening it. "This napkin is sticky! It has chocolate on it." She read out, "One for

Henry." Betsy noticed that the sixth slip of paper had some peanut butter on the outside. "One for Ellen," she said, as she laid it down. The next ballot had a crumb of gingerbread inside it. "One for Richard," Betsy called out. At last she came upon one that was stained with a drop of tomato soup. Betsy knew whose vote it was, but all she said was, "One for Billy."

Billy wrote his name on the list. Betsy said, "That's all."

"Well, what do you know!" said Billy. "What kind of an election is this. Everybody got a vote except Betsy. She didn't get any."

"We'll have to vote over again," said Ellen.

"I can't get another napkin," said Billy. "I had to coax to get this one."

"We can use our own napkins," said Ellen. "Let everybody write down who he wants for president on his own napkin."

"No," said Betsy, "I'm not going to read names off of dirty napkins." Pointing to the pile of little papers, she said, "They were bad enough."

"What do you mean?" asked Kenny.

"Everybody had some of his lunch sticking on his paper," said Betsy.

"I want to vote over again," said Ellen. "I think Betsy should be president. The club was her idea."

"Maybe she doesn't want to be president," said Billy. "Being president of a club is a lot of work."

"What kind of work?" Richard asked.

"Well, well, you have to take care of everything," Billy replied.

"Like what?" asked Henry.

"Well, you have to call meetings," said Billy.

"When are we going to have the meetings?" Mary Lou asked.

"At lunchtime, of course," said Billy. "Right here at lunchtime. Didn't we say this table is for the Friends of Mr. Kilpatrick?"

"The bell calls us to lunch," said Mary Lou.

"How do you want to be called? Do you want the president to call out, 'All the members of the Kilpatrick Club come to lunch?' Or do you want somebody to blow a bugle. We have to go to lunch every day anyway."

"Well, what about the dues?" Billy asked.

"Dues!" exclaimed Ellen. "What are dues for?"

"If you have dues, you have to have a treasurer," said Kenny.

"Let's keep talking about the president," said Betsy. "The bell is going to ring."

Suddenly the bell rang. "Now look!" said Ellen. "There goes the bell, and we haven't elected a president. Everybody who thinks Betsy should be president, hold up your hand."

Every hand at the table went up except Billy's. Then Billy said, "All right. O.K.!" He put up his hand, and added, "It's a lot of work anyway."

Chapter 4

BETSY'S IDEA

THE MEMBERS of the Kilpatrick Club met at their lunch table every day. Nothing was said about Mr. Kilpatrick for some time. The boys were busy talking about their favorite baseball players, and the girls talked a great deal about their hair. Ellen was trying to take the curl *out* of hers; Mary Lou was trying to put curl *into* hers. Betty Jane was letting her hair grow long, and Betsy, having given up pigtails, was feeling pleased with the results.

One day Betsy surprised the children around the table by saying, "Today we are having a meeting of the Kilpatrick Club." Everyone looked up. Betsy continued, "I've been thinking. We should give Mr. Kilpatrick a present when he leaves us."

"We gave him birthday presents once," said Ellen. "And we even had a party for him."

"Yes," said Betsy, "but this present must be the most special present we ever gave him."

"Didn't I tell you we would need dues?" said Billy.

"Will it cost very much money?" asked Ellen.

"No," replied Betsy, very thoughtfully, "not something that costs a lot of money. Something very special."

"Like what?" said Ellen.

"I haven't thought yet," said Betsy, "but I think it should be something alive."

"Alive!" exclaimed Ellen. "Oh, Betsy! That will take a lot of thinking."

"Oh!" cried Billy, suddenly more interested. "Betsy means a dog."

"It ought to be something better than a dog," said Betsy.

"What's better than a dog?" said Billy. "We'll get him a dog."

"Now, Billy, we can't decide anything so important right here while we're eating soup," said Betsy.

"I'm not eating soup," said Billy. "I'm eating sandwiches, but it doesn't make any difference what I eat. Does a person have to eat strawberry shortcake to decide to give Mr. Kilpatrick a dog?"

"We're not going to give Mr. Kilpatrick a dog," Betsy replied.

"What else is there to give him but a dog?" exclaimed Billy. "Don't you know that dogs are called man's best friend? Don't you want to give Mr. Kilpatrick a best friend?"

"Billy!" said Betsy, finishing her soup. "We haven't begun to think yet."

"It takes you an awful long time to think. I can think just like that," he said, snapping his fingers, "and I think of a dog."

"We should form a committee," said Ellen.

"What for?" Billy asked.

"To think," said Ellen.

"That's right," Betsy agreed. "A Think Committee. You can be the chairman, Ellen, because you thought of it."

"She hasn't thought of anything," said Billy. "I thought of a dog."

"She did so think of something," said Betsy, biting into a chocolate brownie. "She thought of a committee."

"Well, all Mr. Kilpatrick needs is a dog," said Billy. "The only thing to decide is what kind of a dog."

"That's easy," said Kenny, who had been eating his sandwich and saying nothing. "We'll give him a police dog."

When the children returned to their classroom, Billy was more enthusiastic than ever about a dog for Mr. Kilpatrick. He kept saying, "That's the thing! That's the present for Mr. Kilpatrick, a police dog."

The last thing Betsy said to him, before Miss Richards called the class to order, was, "We have to think, Billy. We have to think!"

A few days later Betsy and her little sister Star stood alone on the corner, waiting for Mr. Kilpatrick to stop the traffic. When he saw the children, he blew his whistle and held up his hand. Then he beckoned to the children to cross the street. As they reached Mr. Kilpatrick, Betsy stopped beside him and said, "Mr. Kilpatrick, I've been thinking. Wouldn't you like to have some children of your own?"

Mr. Kilpatrick leaned over and said, "How's that again?"

"Wouldn't you and Mrs. Kilpatrick like to have some boys and girls all your own?" said Betsy.

"Well, I don't think I can talk it over with you here in the middle of the street," Mr. Kilpatrick replied. "But if you're thinking of giving me your little sister, nothing would please Mrs. Kilpatrick better than a nice girl like Star. Now run along or I'll have the traffic mad as hornets."

Betsy and Star ran to the other side of the street and walked on to school. When they reached the school yard, Star ran to the first grade children and Betsy joined her own class. Falling into step with Ellen, she said, "I asked Mr. Kilpatrick this morning if he and Mrs. Kilpatrick would

like to have a boy or girl of their own, and he said that they would like one just like Star."

"Well, this morning I'd like to give them my little sister Linda," said Ellen. "She walked backward all the way to school, because she said today was Backwards Day, and I had to keep her from bumping into things. I thought we'd never get here." Ellen pointed to a group of children, and said, "Look at her over there. She even has her hat over her face. Mr. and Mrs. Kilpatrick can certainly have Linda!"

"Oh, your mother wouldn't let her go," said Betsy. "You know she wouldn't."

"No, I guess not," said Ellen. "I guess we're stuck with her."

"A little girl would be a very special kind of present, wouldn't she?" said Betsy.

"A present?" Ellen exclaimed. "Children aren't presents. Presents come wrapped up in fancy paper with a ribbon bow. You can't wrap up a child in fancy paper."

"Of course not, silly," said Betsy, "but there are lots of children who want to be adopted. Don't you look at pictures in magazines? There are always pictures of children who want to be adopted."

"Why do they want to be adopted?" Ellen asked.

"Because they're orphans. They don't have any father or mother," Betsy replied, as she and Ellen went to their seats in their classroom.

The following day Betsy came to school with something to show Ellen. "Wait until you see what I have!" she said, rushing up to Ellen in the school yard.

"What have you got?" Ellen asked.

"Come sit down on the steps," said Betsy, "and I'll show you." The girls sat down, and Betsy opened her schoolbag. She took out a book and inside the cover there was a bit of paper. It had been cut from a magazine. Betsy picked it up

and held it out to Ellen. "I found it in a magazine yesterday," Betsy said. "Isn't it wonderful?"

Ellen took the piece of paper from Betsy and looked at it. It was a photograph of a little girl. "Who is she?" Ellen asked.

"Her name is right there," said Betsy. "It is Ah Ping, and she's Chinese."

"Oh!" said Ellen. "What are you going to do with it?"

"She's the one I told you about," said Betsy. "She wants to be adopted, and I think it would be nice to get her for Mr. and Mrs. Kilpatrick. They would be her foster parents."

"But she's Chinese," said Ellen, "and Mr. and Mrs. Kilpatrick are Irish!"

"Oh, Ellen! What difference does that make? We have some Chinese children right here in our school. We have dark children and light children. Mr. Kilpatrick likes all of us, and now when he goes away he won't have any of us."

"Well, I think she's a very strange present. I

never heard of such a present before," said Ellen, as the school bell rang.

When they reached their classroom, Betsy stopped beside Ellen's desk and whispered, "I wrote to her yesterday."

"Who did you write to?" said Ellen.

"To Ah Ping," Betsy replied. "The little Chinese girl. I told her all about Mr. Kilpatrick."

"Oh, Betsy, you didn't!" exclaimed Ellen. "Without asking Mr. Kilpatrick if he and Mrs. Kilpatrick wanted her?"

"You don't ask people what they want for a present," said Betsy.

"Well, you should have asked me," said Ellen. "I'm chairman of the Think Committee. Everybody will blame it on me."

Miss Richards spoke up and said, "Take your seat, Betsy." Betsy hurried off.

At lunch Billy sat down beside Betsy, and said,

"I've fixed it about the dog for Mr. Kilpatrick. A friend of my father has a German shepherd. She's going to have puppies, and my father's friend says he'll keep one for us. He says we can have it cheap, because it's for Mr. Kilpatrick. The present is all settled."

"Well!" exclaimed Ellen. "I'm chairman of the Think Committee, and we haven't even had a meeting. Billy already has a police dog for Mr. Kilpatrick, and Betsy has a little Chinese girl for him."

"Chinese girl!" exclaimed Billy, Kenny, and Mary Lou all together.

"What do you mean?" said Richard.

"Betsy says the Chinese girl is going to be the present for Mr. Kilpatrick," Ellen replied.

Every member of the Kilpatrick Club stopped eating and looked at Betsy. Kenny turned to her and said, "Are you crazy? What's Mr. Kilpatrick going to do with a Chinese girl?"

"We're going to adopt her for him. Then Mr. and Mrs. Kilpatrick will have a little girl of their own," said Betsy.

"That's the craziest thing I ever heard," said Billy. He was so mad that he picked up his sandwich and left the table. The rest of the club members went on with their lunch, but every once in a while one of them murmured something about the Chinese girl.

When school was over Betsy and Ellen, with their little sisters, walked together toward the corner where Mr. Kilpatrick was standing. As they came closer to him, Ellen said, "Betsy, I think you should ask Mr. Kilpatrick if he wants a little Chinese girl."

"You do?" said Betsy. "If I ask him she won't be a surprise, and anyway I already wrote and told her."

"You shouldn't have," said Ellen. "You should have asked him first."

"Well, all right, I'll ask him," said Betsy.

"What will you do if he doesn't want her?" Ellen asked.

"Oh, when he sees her picture and sees how cute she is, I'm sure he'll want her," Betsy replied.

In a few minutes the children reached Mr. Kilpatrick, and Betsy said, "Mr. Kilpatrick, I have something to show you."

"You have?" said Mr. Kilpatrick. "Well, what is it?"

"It's in my schoolbag," said Betsy. Turning to Ellen, she said, "Here, Ellen, you hold it while I open it." Ellen held the bag while Betsy unfastened the buckles. Then she pulled out a book. "Oh," she said, "that's the wrong one." She put it back and took out another one. "This is it," she said.

Just as Betsy opened the book a gust of wind swept the piece of paper out into the street. It blew across the street right into a culvert where it disappeared from sight. "Oh, dear!" cried Betsy. "Now I've lost it."

"Well, what was it?" Mr. Kilpatrick asked.

"It was a picture of the little Chinese girl, Ah Ping. We were going to adopt her for you and Mrs. Kilpatrick."

"I wasn't. I wasn't," said Ellen. "Just Betsy. I was chairman of the Think Committee, but Betsy didn't give me a chance to think of anything."

"Well, don't worry about that," said Mr. Kilpatrick, not having any idea what Betsy and Ellen were talking about. "No harm's done. I can't speak Chinese anyway, and neither can Mrs. Kilpatrick. Now come along with me to the other side of the street."

Mr. Kilpatrick blew his whistle and held up his hand. The cars stopped, and he led the children to the opposite side. Then he leaned over and said, "I'll tell you some news. I've got a nephew in Ireland, and his house burned down."

"Oh, Mr. Kilpatrick! How terrible!" exclaimed Betsy.

"Did it really?" said Ellen.

"It did really," Mr. Kilpatrick replied. "And him with six children."

"Oh, they weren't burned, were they?" Betsy asked.

"No, they weren't hurt," replied Mr. Kilpatrick, "but he's sending the six children over to stay with Mrs. Kilpatrick and me until he gets his house rebuilt."

"Oh, Mr. Kilpatrick!" exclaimed Betsy. "Isn't that wonderful! Now you and Mrs. Kilpatrick will have children of your own."

"Isn't that grand!" said Mr. Kilpatrick, as he shooed them on their way.

"Well," said Ellen to Betsy, "what are you going to do about that Chinese girl?"

"I don't know," said Betsy. "Maybe she'll have to live with us."

"You'll have to learn to speak Chinese then," said Ellen. "I guess you never thought of that. You shouldn't have written that letter. You shouldn't have thought of it. You should have let the Think Committee think."

Chapter 5

WHO SHOULD CARRY
THE FLAGS?

B ETSY AND Ellen could hardly wait to tell the
others about the children who were coming to stay with the Kilpatricks. As soon as the
club members were gathered around the lunch

77

table, Betsy said, "The meeting will please come to order."

"What?" said Kenny.

"The Kilpatrick Club, of course," said Ellen. "Betsy and I have some news."

"Not that Chinese girl again," said Kenny.

"That's right, Ken," said Henry. "No Chinese girl for Mr. Kilpatrick."

"Don't worry, Hank," said Billy. "We're giving Mr. Kilpatrick a dog. The present is all settled."

"If you didn't make so much noise, I could tell you the news," said Betsy.

"O.K.! What is it?" asked Billy.

"Well," said Betsy, looking very important, "Mr. and Mrs. Kilpatrick are going to have six children."

"All at once?" Mary Lou cried. "How could they have six children all at once?"

"They're coming to live with Mr. and Mrs.

Kilpatrick," said Ellen. "Mr. Kilpatrick told us all about them. Their house burned down."

"Oh, that's great!" said Richard. "I never knew anybody whose house burned down."

"Well, the fire is nothing to be glad about," said Betsy. "How would you feel if your house burned down?"

"I didn't say I was glad about it," said Richard. "I just said I never knew anybody whose house burned down. I hope I can see it."

"You can't," said Ellen, "because the children live in Ireland. They're coming all the way across the Atlantic Ocean."

"They must be coming by airplane," said Billy.

"I guess so," said Ellen, "and I guess Mr. Kilpatrick will go to the airport to meet them. It will be exciting."

"I think we should all go to the airport to meet those poor little children whose house burned down," said Betsy.

"We should ask Mr. Kilpatrick if we can go," said Ellen, remembering that Betsy had not asked about the Chinese girl before writing to her.

"Yes," Betsy agreed. "I think he'll like to have us go to the airport."

"Sure he will!" said Billy, who loved to see the planes come in.

"I guess they'll come in on one of those big jets," said Kenny. "I never met anybody who was flying on a jet."

"We're lucky we have an airport where the jets come in," said Peter.

"What will we do if they come on a day when we are in school?" asked Mary Lou. This remark stopped all talk around the table. No one else had thought of this possibility, and no one liked it.

Finally Billy said, "Well, we'll have to tell Mr. Kilpatrick that the kids must come on a Saturday."

"Oh, sure," said Betsy. "Mr. Kilpatrick will fix it. Mr. Kilpatrick always fixes everything."

"When are they coming?" Henry asked.

"Mr. Kilpatrick didn't tell us, but I guess they will be here soon," said Betsy. "They can't stay in Ireland without a house to live in."

"They belong to Mr. and Mrs. Kilpatrick's nephew," said Ellen.

"I think we should have American flags to wave," said Betsy.

"When?" said Henry.

"When they come," replied Betsy.

"Oh, no!" cried Mary Lou. "We should have Irish flags."

"Of course not," said Billy. "They'll bring their Irish flags with them."

"I never heard of anybody going anyplace with flags," said Betty Jane. "I went in an airplane once, all the way to Florida, and I didn't take a flag with me."

"You stayed in America," said Henry. "If you

had gone to Ireland you would have taken one."

"Why?" Betty Jane asked.

"To show you were an American," said Kenny. "You remember that picture of Christopher Columbus in our history book. He had a flag with him when he got off his boat."

"But Christopher Columbus was discovering America that day. Of course, he had a flag with him," said Henry.

"What kind of a flag?" asked Betty Jane.

"An American flag," Kenny answered.

This reply made Billy laugh very hard. "How could the flag be American?" he said. "Christopher Columbus was just discovering America. He didn't bring an American flag with him. Betsy Ross brought it."

Now Betsy laughed. "Betsy Ross didn't bring an American flag," she said. "Betsy Ross was here. She made the American flag. She made it for George Washington."

"Well, George Washington took it with him

when he crossed the Delaware River," said
Kenny. "The picture is in the history book."

"Soldiers always take flags with them," said
Billy, "but these kids from Ireland aren't soldiers. They won't bring flags with them."

"Then I think we should carry Irish flags
when we go to the airport," said Ellen.

"But, Ellen!" exclaimed Billy. "Where can
we get Irish flags? I don't even know what they
look like."

"That's right," said Kenny. "You have to go
to Ireland to get an Irish flag."

"Sure!" Richard agreed. "We'll have to wait
until the Irish kids come with the Irish flags."

"But if they carry them, how can we wave
them?" Betty Jane asked.

"Betty Jane, you are all mixed up," said Betsy.
"We're going to wave American flags."

"I think we should have both," said Ellen.
"We should have an American flag in one hand
and an Irish flag in the other."

"I don't know where to get an Irish flag," Billy muttered.

That afternoon, when school was over, all of the members of the Kilpatrick Club gathered around the big policeman.

"Mr. Kilpatrick," said Billy, "can we go to the airport when your children come from Ireland?"

"Well!" exclaimed Mr. Kilpatrick. "News travels fast around here. How did you know they were coming by air?"

"Oh, we just guessed," said Kenny.

"But we haven't any Irish flags," said Betty Jane.

"Sure! What do you want Irish flags for?" Mr. Kilpatrick asked.

"To wave when the children get off the plane," said Betty Jane.

"Oh, no!" said Mr. Kilpatrick. "If there's any flag waving, it's the American flag you wave. They're coming to America."

Betty Jane turned to Kenny, and said, "I told you so. Didn't I tell you?" Kenny just grinned.

"Come along now," said Mr. Kilpatrick. "Across the street with all of you."

"Can we go to the airport, Mr. Kilpatrick?" Billy said, as he ran beside the policeman.

"I'll think it over," Mr. Kilpatrick replied.

"When are they coming?" Betsy asked.

"The end of the month," Mr. Kilpatrick answered. "I'm not certain yet what day of the month it will be."

"It has to be on a Saturday," said Billy, when they reached the opposite side of the street. "It has to be Saturday so we can all go to the airport. You will make them come on a Saturday, won't you, Mr. Kilpatrick?"

"I'll see what I can do about it," Mr. Kilpatrick replied. "Sure, it will be a jamboree with the bunch of you to welcome them to America."

Chapter 6

SHARE THE TOYS DAY

T HE DAY Mr. Kilpatrick told the children
that the visitors from Ireland were coming
on the last Saturday of the month, Betsy said,
"Then we can go to the airport to meet them,
can't we, Mr. Kilpatrick?"

"Yes," Mr. Kilpatrick replied. "The children will be glad of such a welcome, but I can't take you. I have to borrow a station wagon from a friend to haul those six children from the airport to my house."

"Oh, that's all right," said Betsy. "My father will take some of us, and I guess Billy's father will take the others."

"Sure!" said Billy, who was standing on the corner beside Betsy.

"Your house will be full of children, won't it, Mr. Kilpatrick?" said Betsy.

"It's the truth you're saying," said Mr. Kilpatrick. "We're building two bunk beds. That takes care of four of them. Where the other two will sleep is a mystery. I guess we'll have to hang them on hooks in the closet. Mrs. Kilpatrick says that she'll be like the old woman who lived in a shoe."

" 'She had so many children, she didn't know

what to do,' " Star sang out, as she skipped beside Mr. Kilpatrick across the street.

"Did the children lose all of their toys in the fire?" Betsy asked Mr. Kilpatrick.

"Everything went up in smoke," he replied. "They'll have to get along without toys."

"And without books?" Betsy asked.

"Yes, without books," Mr. Kilpatrick said.

At lunchtime Betsy said to her friends, "Those poor Irish children lost all their toys and all their books in the fire."

"That's terrible," said Ellen.

"Maybe we could get some toys for them," Mary Lou suggested.

"How?" asked Ellen.

"I don't know, but maybe Miss Richards would have an idea," said Mary Lou.

"They'll have that police-dog puppy to play with," said Billy. "They'll like that puppy better than any toys."

"That puppy isn't even born yet," said Betsy. "Anyway I have my dog Thumpy, but I like dolls. Everyone likes some toys, especially the little children."

"Maybe we could collect toys for them," said Betty Jane.

"Well, let's ask Miss Richards," said Betsy.

After lunch, when the children had returned to their classroom, Betsy raised her hand. "Yes, Betsy?" said Miss Richards.

Betsy stood up. "Miss Richards," she said, "do you know about Mr. Kilpatrick's children who are coming all the way from Ireland to stay with him and Mrs. Kilpatrick?"

"Yes, Betsy. I heard about them," Miss Richards replied. "It's too bad their house burned down, but we'll give them a warm welcome when they come here to school."

"They lost all their toys," said Betsy. "Some of us thought perhaps we could collect some toys for them."

"I think that is an excellent idea," said Miss Richards. "We could have a Share the Toys Day, couldn't we? I'm sure many of you have one toy you could give to these children."

"Sure!" Billy called out. "I can think of one that I could give them." Many children in the class nodded their head.

"What about books?" Richard asked.

"Books would be fine, too," Miss Richards replied.

"I've got a toy dump truck that I could give them," said Kenny.

"Everyone doesn't have to bring a toy," said Miss Richards. "Some of you can help in other ways. Perhaps a few of the toys will need a new coat of paint or perhaps they should be repaired. Let's see how many children would like to have a Share the Toys Day." Every hand in the class went up.

Peter raised his hand, and said, "I don't have any toy that I can bring, but I can make something. I know how to make a cart out of a wooden box and some empty spools. I could do that if I had a box."

"I have a box I can give you, Peter," said Miss Richards.

"I don't have any toy either," said Ellen, "but I can make a doll out of old stockings. My grandmother showed me how. But I guess that wouldn't be sharing, would it, Miss Richards?"

"Indeed making a doll would be sharing," Miss Richards replied. "You would be sharing your talent."

"Is making a doll out of old stockings a talent?" Ellen asked, laughing a bit. "I thought talent was playing the piano or painting a beautiful picture."

"Talent is doing anything well," said Miss Richards, "and to do anything well you have to love doing it. Then the talent grows."

Share the Toys Day was set for the Monday before the Irish children were due to arrive. Miss

Richards kept her promise to Peter and brought a wooden box to school so that he could make a wagon. A few days later Billy came to school with a toy horse to go with the wagon. Peter was delighted, for the horse was just the right size. He made the wagon in school, and all the children watched it grow from a little wooden box to a wagon with a horse. They saw Peter attach the wheels and make the shafts from wooden sticks. He finished it with a coat of bright red paint.

While Peter was making the wagon, Ellen was turning some old stockings into a doll. She made the head and the body out of a pair of white stockings that her grandmother had dyed a soft shade of pink. Ellen stuffed the doll with cotton. She sewed two blue buttons on the face for eyes and a bit of red felt for the mouth. The nose and the eyebrows she made with brown paint. She made the hair from yellow yarn and fastened it to the top of the doll's head.

Betsy offered to make a dress for the doll, and Mary Lou made a hat. The blue-and-white checked dress and the floppy hat looked very attractive when they were finished, and Betsy added little black socks to cover the doll's feet to complete the costume.

Ellen's doll and Peter's wagon were finished on the same day. Before the children left school the horse and wagon and the doll were placed side by side on one of the windowsills. They were all ready for Share the Toys Day.

The next morning Betsy arrived at school with a large picture book under her arm. Nearly every child was carrying a toy or a book. They held them up for each other to see. There were all kinds of toys. Toys for boys and toys for girls. Some were very tiny, and some, like Christopher's toy bear, were very big. Some of the toys were old and many of the books were worn, but all the toys and all the books looked as though someone had loved them.

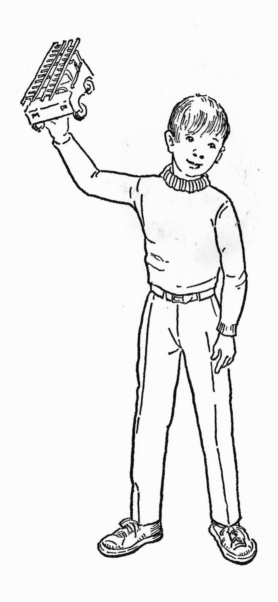

The children came into their room with beaming faces. They were all anxious to show the gifts they had brought with them to Miss Richards. When she looked around the room, she said, "What lovely gifts you've brought. I'm sure the six little Kilpatricks will be delighted."

"Mine needs a little paint," said Richard, holding up a fire engine.

"My tin clown needs a screw in his arm," said Henry. "When you wind him up he can walk across the room. Do you think we can fix his arm?"

"We can make all of the repairs that are needed," Miss Richards replied.

Peter's eyes had been roving over the windowsills. He raised his hand, and said, "Miss Richards, where did you put my horse and wagon?"

Miss Richards looked across the room to the windowsills. The children's eyes followed hers. Most of the children stood up in order to see better. There was nothing on the windowsills.

"I didn't move them," said Miss Richards. "Perhaps Mr. Jones, our new janitor, put them away when he cleaned the room yesterday. I'll ring for him."

Miss Richards pushed the button to call Mr. Jones. When he came into the room, Miss Richards said, "Mr. Jones, some toys were left on the windowsill yesterday. Perhaps you put them somewhere when you cleaned the room."

Mr. Jones scratched his head, and said, "I don't recall seeing any toys on the windowsill. What kind of toys were they?"

"A horse and wagon," said Peter, looking very troubled.

"And Ellen's doll," said Betsy. "She had a blue-and-white checked dress and a hat."

"Don't recollect seeing them at all," said Mr. Jones. "I would have seen them when I dusted the windowsills, and I know I dusted them." Mr. Jones shook his head and looked very puzzled.

"Thank you, Mr. Jones," said Miss Richards.

"I'm sure we'll find them." Mr. Jones went out of the room, leaving puzzled faces behind him. Where had the toys gone?

Miss Richards spoke to the children. "When everyone has put his toy or book on the table in the back of the room, we can all look inside our desks," she said. The children carried the toys and books to the back of the room, and soon the table was covered with gifts for the Kilpatrick boys and girls.

The children spent ten minutes hunting through their desks. They found many things to throw into the wastepaper basket, but the cart and the horse and the doll were not found. Betsy and Ellen looked in one of the closets; Peter and Billy looked in another. Miss Richards looked in her own closet, but the lost toys did not come to light.

Finally Peter said, "Maybe the toys are out with the rubbish." He looked out the window, and said, "The rubbish cans are still in back.

We could look in them and see if the toys are there."

"Oh, Peter!" said Miss Richards. "You can't spend the day going through all of that rubbish."

"Couldn't I just have ten minutes to look?" Peter asked. "Maybe they're right on top."

"Very well," said Miss Richards, "ten minutes only."

Peter put on his jacket and left the room. "I hope he finds them," said Ellen. "It took me a long time to make that doll."

Peter walked through the long corridor toward the back door. As he passed the library he looked in the door, which was open. Miss Stevens, the librarian, was sitting at her desk examining some new books. A long table stood at the front of the room. It was the table that Miss Stevens used for exhibits. Peter glanced at it, and there, to his great surprise, he saw his horse and cart standing in front of a group of books. At the other end of the table he saw

Ellen's doll sitting in front of some other books.

Peter walked into the library. Miss Stevens looked up, and said, "Hello, Peter! What can I do for you?"

Peter was so relieved to see his cart and Ellen's doll that he could hardly get any words out. Finally he stammered, "Well, well, I think that's my horse and cart."

"Oh, I didn't know it was yours, Peter!" said Miss Stevens. "I asked Miss Richards if I could borrow something for the book exhibit. She had gone home when I went to her room, and I thought she had left the horse and cart and the doll on the windowsill for me."

"Oh!" exclaimed Peter. "I was just about to go through the rubbish." Peter pointed out the window at the rubbish cans.

"I'm sorry," said Miss Stevens. "Come! We'll take them back to your room." Peter picked up his horse and cart, and Miss Stevens carried the doll. When they reached Miss Richards' room, everyone laughed when they heard what had happened to Peter's cart and Ellen's doll.

When the cart and the doll had been placed on the table with the rest of the toys, the whole class settled down. The room was very quiet the rest of the morning.

Chapter 7

THE ARRIVAL

ON FRIDAY afternoon the children packed all the toys and books into a large box. Billy had brought his express wagon to school, and Peter helped Billy put the box in the wagon. Betsy wrote a card to tie on the box. It said, "Wel-

come to the Kilpatrick children from Miss Richards' class."

Betsy said to Billy, "I think I should help to
pull the wagon, because I am president of the
Kilpatrick Club."

"O.K.!" said Billy.

At the end of the day, when the bell rang, all
the children lined up behind Billy and Betsy and
the express wagon. Everyone in the class wanted
to take the box of toys to Mr. Kilpatrick. As
soon as they were outside of school, they formed
a large bunch with Billy and Betsy and the express wagon in the middle. Suddenly Billy said
to Betsy, "Say! Maybe these Kilpatrick kids
don't speak English."

"Of course, they speak English," Betsy replied. "Mr. Kilpatrick speaks English."

"I know," said Billy, "but Mr. Kilpatrick has
been in this country for ages."

Soon the crowd of children reached the corner
where Mr. Kilpatrick was standing. When he

saw Miss Richards' whole class, he said, "What's the celebration going on here? If it's a parade, I'll have to arrest you because you can't hold a parade without a permit." Mr. Kilpatrick laughed, and everyone knew he was joking.

"It's for your children, Mr. Kilpatrick," said Betsy. "We've brought some toys for them."

"They're in this box," said Billy.

"They're from all of us in Miss Richards' room," said Kenny.

"Not just from the Kilpatrick Club," said Ellen.

"The what?" said Mr. Kilpatrick.

"The Kilpatrick Club," said Betsy. "Didn't you know about the Kilpatrick Club?"

"Sure, I never thought I'd be so famous as to have a club named after me," said Mr. Kilpatrick. "I'll bet there's nobody on the whole police force with a club named for him."

"Oh, you're the most famous policeman in this whole town," said Billy.

"Well, all you boys and girls giving up your toys for the children is mighty fine," said Mr. Kilpatrick. "These gifts will be a wonderful welcome for them."

"I wrote *welcome* on the card," said Betsy, pointing to the card she had tied on the box.

"Can they read English, Mr. Kilpatrick?" Billy asked.

"Sure, they can read English," Mr. Kilpatrick replied.

"And do they speak English?" Ellen asked.

"Of course!" Mr. Kilpatrick answered. "But they speak Gaelic too."

"What's that they speak?" Kenny asked.

"Gaelic!" said Mr. Kilpatrick. "It's the Irish tongue. If you want to welcome somebody in Gaelic, you say, *Céad míle Fáilte.*" The expression sounded like *cayed meeleh foilteh.*

"What do those words mean?" Betsy asked.

"They mean a hundred thousand welcomes," said Mr. Kilpatrick.

"Oh, Mr. Kilpatrick!" exclaimed Betsy. "That is a great big welcome!"

"A hundred thousand!" said Billy. "Whee!"

"That's a much bigger welcome than I wrote on this card," said Betsy. "Could you write it on this card, Mr. Kilpatrick?"

Mr. Kilpatrick took a pencil from his pocket. He leaned down and wrote, "Céad míle Fáilte."

"That will make them feel welcome, won't it, Mr. Kilpatrick?" said Kenny, who had pushed his way through the crowd and was standing by the wagon.

"Oh, they'll feel welcome all right," said Mr. Kilpatrick, as he lifted the box out of Billy's wagon. He carried it to his red car and placed it on the front seat. "I can't thank you enough for these gifts," he called out to the children. "Thank you very, very much for being so good to the children."

All of the boys and girls called back, "You're welcome." Then the children scattered in every direction. A large number crossed the street with Mr. Kilpatrick. When Betsy and Billy reached the other side, they said to Mr. Kilpatrick, "See you tomorrow at the airport."

"I'll be looking for you," Mr. Kilpatrick replied.

The plane, bringing the Kilpatrick children from Ireland, was due at the airport at two o'clock in the afternoon. Betsy's father was to pick up the girls, and Billy's father was to pick up the boys. All members of the Kilpatrick Club were going to welcome the Irish children.

When Betsy's father arrived at Ellen's house, Betsy and Star were both on the front seat. Linda and Ellen got into the back. "Isn't it exciting?" said Ellen, as she settled herself.

"Oh, yes!" Betsy replied. "I hope everybody gets there in time to see the plane come in. I hope the boys won't be late."

Betsy's father made two more stops. He picked

up Mary Lou and Betty Jane. They both climbed into the back of the car with Ellen and Linda.

The moment Betty Jane got into the car, she said, "What about the flags? Are we going to have flags to wave?"

"Oh, yes!" Betsy replied. "Billy is bringing the flags."

Ellen leaned over the back of the front seat, and said, "Betsy, did you ever get a letter from Ah Ping?"

"From whom?" Betsy asked.

"From Ah Ping," Ellen repeated. "You know, the little Chinese girl you wrote to."

"Oh, her!" said Betsy. "No, I never heard from her."

"I guess she never got that letter," said Ellen.

When the girls reached the airport, they found the boys already there. They were lined up at the big windows watching the planes coming in and going out. Betsy noticed that there was a large man and a plump little woman in the group. She wondered who they were, and suddenly she realized that they were Mr. and Mrs. Kilpatrick. She had never seen Mr. Kilpatrick dressed in anything except his policeman's uniform, and she had never seen Mrs. Kilpatrick wearing a hat before.

"Oh, Mr. Kilpatrick!" said Betsy. "I didn't know you. You look different when you haven't your uniform on." Then she added, "You look very nice, and I like Mrs. Kilpatrick's hat."

Mrs. Kilpatrick looked pleased, and Mr. Kilpatrick said, "Thank you, Betsy. I never saw you wearing green ribbons before."

"They're for the Irish children," said Betsy. "Green is for Ireland, isn't it, Mr. Kilpatrick?"

"It is, indeed," Mr. Kilpatrick replied.

Mr. Kilpatrick walked up and down and up and down, looking at his watch again and again. Mrs. Kilpatrick kept saying to him, "Oh, do try to be quiet, Pat."

Mr. Kilpatrick kept saying to her, "I never had six children before. Six children! All at once! It's something to make a man a little jumpy."

Suddenly there was a voice on the loudspeaker saying, "Flight Number 82 from Shannon, Ireland, arriving at Gate Number Three. This flight will continue to Washington, D.C."

When Betsy heard this announcement, she felt a tingling sensation all the way down her back. She pressed her nose against the windowpane, and said to Ellen, who was beside her, "Oh! This is the most exciting thing I ever did."

"Me too. My hands are all wet," said Ellen.

"There it is! There it is!" Billy and Kenny shouted together.

Then all the boys pointed to the big jet that was coming in from the runway. "That's it!" they cried. "Here it is!"

The children watched the jet as it came closer and closer to the berth. It moved slowly and smoothly until it finally stopped right in front of the window where the children were standing. Quickly the steps were pushed out to the plane, the steps, thought Betsy, that the children would come down. She wondered whether she would know which ones were the Kilpatrick children.

Suddenly Betty Jane called out, "The flags! The flags! We haven't got the flags!"

Billy dropped the box he had been holding under this arm. "Oh! I forgot the flags!" he said.

Betty Jane and Mary Lou both tried to help Billy untie the knot around the box, but Betsy's eyes were glued to the door of the plane. She hardly noticed when Betty Jane put a flag in her hand, for the door had opened. Betsy watched for the first passenger to come down the steps. Would it be one of the Irish children or would it be someone else?

It was someone else. It was a little girl, but Betsy could see that she was not Irish. She was Chinese. Betsy could see very clearly that she was Chinese. Her hands turned as cold as ice. Six Irish children were coming to live with Mr. and Mrs. Kilpatrick, and here was a Chinese girl!

Ellen saw the child too. "Oh, Betsy!" she cried. "There is Ah Ping!"

"Oh, Ellen!" Betsy whispered, for her voice seemed to have left her. "What shall we do with her?"

"I told you that you shouldn't have written that letter," said Ellen.

Suddenly Mr. Kilpatrick called out, "There they are! That's them!"

All the children around Betsy and Ellen began waving the American flags and calling out, "That's them!"

Betsy was too upset to wave her flag, but she took her eyes away from the Chinese girl long enough to look back at the plane. She saw six children, of different ages, coming down the steps. At the bottom they gathered in a tight knot and moved toward the entrance to the airport.

Betsy looked again for the Chinese girl. She was standing alone right below the window where Betsy and Ellen were. She seemed to be waiting. "Oh! What shall I do?" Betsy whispered to Ellen.

"I guess she's waiting for Mr. Kilpatrick," said Ellen.

Betsy looked around for Mr. Kilpatrick, but both Mr. and Mrs. Kilpatrick had disappeared. Betsy looked back at the Chinese girl. She was still waiting. Betsy's eyes returned to the steps beside the plane. Then she saw a Chinese woman and a Chinese man come down the steps. The little girl ran to meet them, and the woman took hold of the child's hand. Betsy gave a big sigh of relief. She wasn't Ah Ping after all! This little girl was not alone. Betsy lifted her arm high and waved her flag.

"Betsy!" exclaimed Billy. "Why are you wav-

ing the flag now? Why didn't you wave your flag when we were waving?"

"I'm waving, because I'm happy," Betsy replied.

"The kids have gone inside," said Billy.

"Mr. Kilpatrick says they won't be out here for at least fifteen minutes," said Kenny. "He and Mrs. Kilpatrick have gone to help them with their suitcases and things."

"Don't forget to wave the flags when they come," said Billy.

The children waited with Billy's father and Betsy's. They stood close to the door through which the Irish children would walk with Mr. and Mrs. Kilpatrick.

After a while the door opened, and Mrs. Kilpatrick appeared with two little twin girls. They had bright red curls all over their heads. Behind them came a girl about Betsy's age. She had big blue eyes and long dark hair, and she was leading another little girl by the hand. This one had dark red hair like Betsy's. Two boys followed with Mr. Kilpatrick. There was a boy a little bigger than Billy and one about six years old.

"Well, here we are!" said Mr. Kilpatrick. Then he said to the Irish children, "Now suppose you all stand in a line, and I'll introduce you to your new friends who have come to meet you."

The six Irish children lined up, the biggest at one end and the twins at the other. Mr. Kilpatrick started with the first boy in the line. "This is Cormac," he said, "and this blue-eyed colleen is Nora." Mr. Kilpatrick chucked the next one under her chin, and said, "And this colleen is Bridget. Then we have the little brother Brian." Last he reached the twins. He put his hand on one of the curly red heads, and said, "This is Kathleen and her twin Eileen."

Then Mr. Kilpatrick introduced the members of the Kilpatrick Club and Linda and Star. When he had finished he said to the Irish children, "Sure, you're lucky children to have such fine new friends." In a moment the children were all together. The Irish children had the American flags, and the big crowd of children walked to the cars that were to take them home. Everyone waved good-bye as the cars started. The Irish children waved the flags.

"They're nice," said Betsy.

"Yes," said Ellen, "but I don't know where the Colleens come in."

"What do you mean?" Betsy asked.

"Well," said Ellen, "Mr. Kilpatrick called two of those girls Colleen. They can't both be Colleen."

Chapter 8

BRIAN'S LEPRECHAUN

THE FOLLOWING Monday the six Kilpatrick children came to school. Nora and Cormac were both in Betsy's class, although Nora was a little younger and Cormac was a little older. Bridget was in the second grade with

Linda. The twins were in the kindergarten, and Brian was in the first grade with Star. At lunchtime Nora sat at the table between Betsy and Ellen, and Billy and Kenny made room for Cormac. The younger children had an earlier lunch.

The first thing that Nora said when she was seated at the table was, "Cormac is writing a letter to the class for giving us all those lovely toys. We'll sign the letter after he writes it. Such beautiful toys! It was kind of everybody, wasn't it, Cormac?"

"Oh, very kind!" said Cormac. "Very kind, it was. Little Brian took to the red cart with the horse right away."

"Do you like being in America?" Ellen asked.

"It seems very nice," Nora replied. "And you have a fine school."

"And those bunk beds that we have at Uncle's!" said Cormac. "They're something we've never seen before."

"Mr. Kilpatrick said he would have to hang two of you on hooks in the closet," Betsy said, laughing. "Which ones hang on the hooks?"

"Oh, we're not quite that squeezed," said Cormac, "but Nora and Bridget have to sleep on cots in the parlor."

"Did your home in Ireland really burn down to the ground?" Kenny asked.

"It did," Cormac replied, "but my father is building another one for us."

"And it will be better than the first," said Nora. "It just takes a wee bit of time."

"A wee bit!" said Billy. "I should think building it would take a big bit."

"Oh, time is all the same!" said Nora. "We always have plenty of time in Ireland."

"It's the truth!" said Cormac. "An Irish lad can spend a whole day and night just looking for leprechauns."

"Looking for what?" Billy asked.

"Leprechauns!" Cormac replied. "Do you not have wee folk in this country?"

"What are wee folk?" Ellen asked.

"Fairies!" said Nora. "But the leprechauns are the true Irish variety."

"Did you ever see one?" Kenny asked.

"No, I never did," Cormac replied. "They're hard to find and even harder to catch. A person can only find them in the full of the moon, and they get away by playing tricks. Very tricky, leprechauns!"

"What do they look like?" Billy asked.

"Well, they're little green men, so much the color of leaves that it's hard to see them. Now if you're so fortunate as to see one, you'll find him making shoes, because all leprechauns are cobblers."

"Who do they make them for?" asked Betsy.

"Why for the leprechauns, of course!" Cormac answered.

"Did you ever find any leprechaun shoes?" Betsy wanted to know.

"No, never," said Cormac. "As I said, the leprechauns are very hard to find. Most people don't know how to catch a leprechaun."

"How do you catch them?" Betsy asked.

"There's only one way," said Cormac. "By his ear."

"You mean he's something like a rabbit?" asked Betsy.

"Oh, no!" Cormac replied. "Not at all."

"Why do people want to catch them?" Ellen asked.

"For the bag of gold that every leprechaun has with him," Cormac replied. "Now Brian, that's my little brother, says he caught one and that he's brought it with him in his little bag."

"Oh, he hasn't!" Ellen cried. "Leprechauns aren't real. They're just fairies."

"I only know what my brother Brian says,"

said Cormac. "He told me he couldn't be going to America without a leprechaun."

"Have you seen it?" Betsy asked.

"No," said Cormac, "he hasn't showed it to me."

"But how do you know he has one, if you haven't seen it?" Billy asked.

"Sure, if my brother Brian says he's got a leprechaun, he's got it. I don't have to see everything my brother Brian sees," said Cormac. "Maybe my brother Brian has better eyesight than I have. Why should I doubt what he sees?"

"But maybe he's making it up," said Ellen. "Maybe it's just in his mind."

"Maybe," said Cormac, "but I'm not one for taking his leprechaun away from him, because I haven't seen it. Leprechauns are very important to some people, and they are very important to Brian. I say let him have his leprechaun. It's as real as any leprechaun in Ireland and don't any

of you go telling him he doesn't have a leprechaun."

All the children had been sitting with their
eyes on Cormac's face. When he finished speak-
ing, they looked at each other. Finally Betsy
said, "You know, I like these leprechauns. Now
that the Kilpatricks have come, I think we should
change the name of our club to the Leprechaun
Club, and they can be members too."

"That's a good idea," Billy agreed.

"All right!" said Betsy. "All in favor hold up
your hand." Every child around the table held
up his hand just as the bell rang.

When school was out, Betsy met Brian at Mr.
Kilpatrick's corner. Brian was standing alone
beside Mr. Kilpatrick's red car. He was holding
a small plaid bag. "Hello, Brian!" said Betsy.

"Hello!" said Brian.

"What have you got in your bag?" asked
Betsy.

"Shush!" whispered Brian. "He's asleep."

"Who's asleep?" said Betsy.

Brian whispered again, "My leprechaun."

"Couldn't I peep at him?" Betsy asked.

"Well," said Brian, "you can have a quick look." Brian opened the bag very carefully. He did not open it very wide. "I would not open it at all," he said, "if he were awake. I might lose him."

Betsy leaned over and looked into the bag. "Do you see him?" Brian asked.

"Oh, he's lovely!" said Betsy.

"Do you see the gold lace on his three-cornered hat?" Brian asked.

"It's beautiful," said Betsy.

"And do you see that bag of gold he has?" Brian asked.

"Imagine a leprechaun having a bag of gold like that!" said Betsy.

"It's quite heavy," said Brian. "And do you see the pair of shoes he's making? Not now, of course, because he's taking his nap."

"Oh, they'll be nice shoes when he finishes them," Betsy answered.

Just then Mr. Kilpatrick came over to the children. "Brian has been showing me his leprechaun," said Betsy.

"Has he now!" said Mr. Kilpatrick, stooping down and looking into Brian's bag. Then Mr. Kilpatrick looked at Betsy, and said, "Sure now, Betsy, what are you thinking?"

"I'm thinking it's a very fine specimen of a leprechaun," Betsy replied.

Mr. Kilpatrick straightened up. He smiled down at Betsy, and said, "Sure, Betsy! You're my darlin'!"

Chapter 9

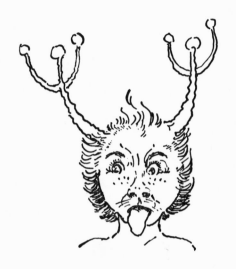

BEDTIME STORIES

WHEN BETSY got home from school, she found her mother in the kitchen making an apple pie. Betsy sat down on a kitchen stool, and said, "Mother, those Kilpatrick children are so nice, and they know all about fairies and leprechauns. They're wonderful kids!"

"I'm glad you have some more friends," her mother said. "Tell me about them."

"Well, there's Nora who's a little younger than I, and Cormac who's a little older."

"So you are the cheese in the sandwich?" said her mother.

Betsy laughed. "That's right," she agreed. "Then there are the twins. I think they're only five. Anyway, they're in kindergarten. Brian is six, and he's a funny little boy. He has a make-believe leprechaun that he carries around in a plaid bag. Of course, we all make believe it's real. After all, when someone is far away he likes to have something that reminds him of home. The leprechaun reminds Brian of Ireland."

"I'm sure the leprechaun comforts Brian," said her mother.

"Then there's Bridget. She's in second grade with Linda," said Betsy. "Bridget is so cute."

"I'm looking forward to meeting these children," said Betsy's mother. "Your father says the girls are very pretty."

"Oh, they are, Mother!" said Betsy. "They don't talk the way we do. They sort of sing when they talk." Betsy ate a piece of apple. Then she said, "The Kilpatrick's house must be very crowded. Nora and Bridget have to sleep on cots in the parlor. I was thinking, Mother, couldn't Nora and Bridget come and live with us? I have an extra bed in my room, and there's an empty bunk above Star's bed."

Betsy's mother thought about this suggestion for a few minutes, and then she said, "I think that's a very good idea, Betsy."

"Goody!" cried Betsy, jumping off the stool. "Will you go call up Mrs. Kilpatrick? Will you call her right now?"

"We'd better call your father first," said Mother, "and see if he wants two more little girls."

"Well, call him, Mother!" said Betsy. "Do call him."

"As soon as I get this pie in the oven I'll call him," her mother replied.

Betsy ran off to find Star. She found her lying on the floor in the living room with crayons and a coloring book. "Star," she said, "would you like Bridget and Nora to come and live with us? Bridget would sleep in the bunk over your bed."

"O.K.," said Star, without looking up. "I'm making this tree purple."

"You should make it green," said Betsy.

"I like purple trees," said Star. "It's an orange tree, and it has purple oranges."

"But oranges are orange, Star, not purple," said Betsy.

"I like purple oranges," said Star, "and purple orange juice."

Betsy laughed. "You like to play make believe, the way Brian plays with his leprechaun."

"What's a leprechaun?" Star asked.

"An Irish fairy," replied Betsy.

"Is he purple?" Star asked.

"No, he's green," Betsy replied.

"Then I wouldn't like him," said Star. "I'd only like him if he were purple."

Betsy heard her mother dialing a telephone number. She ran into the hall where the telephone stood on the hall table. "Star's all purple today," she said to her mother. "She doesn't like anything that isn't purple."

Betsy stood beside her mother while she talked with Betsy's father. Betsy was so close to the telephone that she could hear her father's voice. He said to her mother, "It's all right with me, if it's all right with you." Betsy began to dance around in a circle.

When her mother hung up the receiver, she said, "You heard, didn't you, Betsy?"

"Oh, yes!" Betsy replied. "Now can we please call Mrs. Kilpatrick?"

Betsy's mother looked in the telephone book

for the number under the name, Kilpatrick. When she found it she dialed it right away. In a few moments Mrs. Kilpatrick answered. Betsy's mother didn't have to talk very long before she persuaded Mrs. Kilpatrick to let Nora and Bridget come to stay with Betsy and Star.

"I'll have to speak to Mr. Kilpatrick," said Mrs. Kilpatrick. "He's just about to go out. Will you please hold the phone a minute?"

Betsy and her mother waited while Mrs. Kilpatrick spoke to her husband. "I do hope they can come," said Betsy.

Soon Mrs. Kilpatrick was on the telephone again. "Mr. Kilpatrick and I have talked it over, and we've spoken to the girls, and we accept your lovely invitation. You are very kind to take Nora and Bridget."

"Can they come this afternoon?" said Betsy, poking her mother. Her mother repeated the question to Mrs. Kilpatrick. When she hung up the receiver, she said, "They'll be ready to come before dinner. We'll go over for them."

"That's wonderful!" said Betsy.

About five o'clock Betsy and Star climbed into the car beside their mother. Off they went to get Nora and Bridget. The two girls were waiting for them when they reached the Kilpatricks'. Their suitcase was standing by the front door.

Mrs. Kilpatrick helped them into their coats. "Oh, you are so kind," she said to Betsy's mother. "They'll be good children, I'm sure."

Turning to Nora, she said, "Now you take care of Bridget and do be helpful in the home. Comb Bridget's hair, see that she keeps her hands clean and that she cleans her teeth. Wash out your own stockings and Bridget's. Make your own beds and keep your things tidy. Wash Bridget's hair when you wash your own every week. Keep your nails clean and trim Bridget's toenails or she'll get holes in her stockings."

"I will, Aunt," Nora kept saying. "I will."

"See that Bridget uses her napkin, and don't spot the tablecloth," Mrs. Kilpatrick continued, as she followed them to the front door. "If it turns cold, be sure to button up, and see that Bridget says her prayers."

"I will, Aunt," Nora replied. "I'll remember."

"Mother hears our prayers," said Betsy. "She'll hear Bridget's and Nora's, too. Won't you, Mother?"

"Of course, I will," her mother replied. Then she said to Mrs. Kilpatrick, "Don't worry about them, Mrs. Kilpatrick. We'll all get along fine."

When Nora and Bridget kissed Mrs. Kilpatrick good-bye, she said, "Your uncle will be sorry he couldn't kiss you good-bye, but you'll see him in the morning at the usual place." She followed the children out to the car. Then she said to Betsy's mother, "You have no idea what a help you are being to me. I love having the children, but the house does seem to be bursting its sides."

Just as the car was about to start, Mr. Kilpatrick walked up. "Well! I see you've come for my little colleens."

"Mr. Kilpatrick," Betsy asked, "why do you call all of the girls Colleen?"

Mr. Kilpatrick laughed. "Oh, *colleen* is the Irish word for little girl," he said.

"Oh!" cried Betsy. "Am I a colleen?"

"You are, indeed!" Mr. Kilpatrick replied.

"Me, too?" Star asked.

"You too, Twinkle," said Mr. Kilpatrick. Turning to Betsy's mother, he said, "I'll miss Nora and Bridget, but they will be more comfortable with you, and I do appreciate your kindness."

Then Mr. Kilpatrick kissed Nora and Bridget. In a moment Betsy's mother was off with the four girls.

That night, long after Star and Bridget were sound asleep, Betsy and Nora sat up in their beds talking. Nora told Betsy all about their house that had burned down in Ireland. "It was the thatched roof that caught fire," said Nora.

"What is a thatched roof?" Betsy asked.

"It's a roof made of straw," replied Nora. "Very thick, it is."

"Tell me," said Betsy, "what is flying across the ocean like?"

"Oh, it's grand!" Nora replied. "It's like having a magic carpet. I sat back and closed my eyes, and I said to myself, 'Now I'm flying on my magic carpet.'"

"You make a fairy tale out of everything, don't you?" said Betsy.

"Oh, I guess you can say that," said Nora. "We're never far from the wee folk." Nora threw back the blanket on her bed, and said, "My, I never was in such a warm house." Then she hastened to add, "I'm not complaining, mind you. It's grand, but you must be cutting peat all the time to keep it so cozy."

"Cutting what?" Betsy asked.

"Peat!" Nora replied. "What you burn to heat the house."

"We heat the house with gas," said Betsy. "Pipes bring it in from the street."

"Oh!" said Nora. "In Ireland we have to go to the peat bogs and cut the peat."

"What does it look like?" Betsy asked.

"It looks like dark brown earth," Nora replied. "Sometimes it's black."

"Do you mean you burn dirt to heat your house!" Betsy exclaimed.

"Well, it's not like dirt," said Nora. "It's thick and sometimes sticky, and we cut it in blocks. Then it has to dry out. You see it piled up all over the country. It's very good for burning."

"I never saw any in this country," said Betsy.

"Oh, many's the time I've gone with my daddy to the peat bog. He takes the wagon, and we all ride back on the load of peat."

"Isn't it awfully dirty?" Betsy asked.

"Oh, sure! We come home looking like chimney sweeps," said Nora. She lowered her voice, and added, "I'd never go near the peat bogs at night, though, especially if there's a full moon in the sky."

"Why not?" Betsy asked.

"Because the pucas hide in the peat bogs, and when the moon is full they come out. No person but half a fool would go to the peat bogs in the moonlight."

"What's a puca?" Betsy asked. "Is he some kind of a leprechaun?"

"Oh, no!" Nora replied. "A puca is a nasty little beast. He has two long horns on the side of his head, and if you're thinking of picking him up, you grab him by his horns."

"Oh! I wouldn't want to pick up one," said Betsy.

"Well, as Cormac was saying the other day," said Nora, "leprechauns are tricky, but they'll never sneak up on you. If you're so fortunate as to come upon a leprechaun, you'll find him sitting quiet. He'll either be counting his gold or making a pair of shoes. But a puca! Ah, there's a sneaky one! He knows that you'll catch him by his horns if he meets you head on, so he sneaks up on you very, very quiet like."

At this moment the bathroom door squeaked. Betsy felt her toes turn up. She listened for the door to squeak again, but everything was quiet. Thumpy, Betsy's cocker spaniel, must have pushed the door open.

Nora continued. "Now the trickiest of all the tricky is the banshee. A banshee is a little witch, and she will scare you so that you would run up the wall of Blarney castle to get away from her.

There's nothing quiet about her. A person may be walking along just singing to himself, when suddenly—*Bang!*—there's a banshee!" Just as Nora cried *"Bang!"* there was a terrible bang against the window right beside Betsy's bed.

"E-e-e-k!" Betsy cried out, and dived under the covers. She crawled all the way to the bottom of the bed. She waited. There was no other sound, so she lifted up the covers and called out to Nora, "Is it gone?"

"Sure, it was just a shutter on the window that banged," Nora replied.

"Weren't you scared?" asked Betsy, crawling back to her pillow.

"Oh, no!" Nora replied. "I knew it was no banshee. They're home in Ireland, and there's not a magic carpet among all the banshees in Ireland."

"I guess we'd better go to sleep now," said Betsy.

"Yes," replied Nora, "and right cozy it is in

this bed." In a few moments she said, "I hope that banshee didn't waken Bridget!"

Betsy shuddered and turned her face away from the window, but soon she was fast asleep.

Chapter 10

SURPRISES

ONE MORNING late in October, when Betsy went downstairs, she saw a white envelope lying on the hall table. Betsy thought at once that it might be an invitation to a party, so she picked it up. She looked at it carefully and saw the name and address. Then she called out, "Mother!"

Her mother answered from the dining room, "Yes, Betsy. What is it?"

Betsy came into the dining room, where Nora was helping to set the table. She held up the letter. "Mother!" she said. "This letter! It was on the hall table!"

"Yes," her mother replied. "I found that letter in the pocket of your father's raincoat. The address is in your handwriting, but I didn't know that you had a friend in Hong Kong."

"Oh, Mother!" said Betsy. "I asked Father to mail this letter. I gave it to him weeks ago."

"Well, your father hasn't had his raincoat on for weeks," said her mother. "I'm sending it to the cleaners today, and I looked in all the pockets. It's too bad he forgot to mail your letter, but do tell me about your Chinese friend in Hong Kong."

"I don't know anyone in Hong Kong," said

Betsy. "I saw Ah Ping's picture in one of your magazines, and I thought our club would adopt her for Mr. and Mrs. Kilpatrick, because they didn't have any children of their own. Mr. Kilpatrick was leaving, and I knew he would miss all the children in our school. The magazine said that Ah Ping needed foster parents and Mr. and Mrs. Kilpatrick would be wonderful foster parents. Of course, I didn't know about the Kilpatrick children coming from Ireland."

Betsy's mother stood listening to this long speech, and when Betsy stopped for breath, she said, "Betsy! You sometimes get the strangest ideas."

"Well, when I saw a Chinese girl get off the plane with Nora and her brothers and sisters, I was very scared," said Betsy. "I thought Ah Ping had come. She would have mixed things up a bit, wouldn't she, Mother?"

"She would indeed have mixed things up a bit," her mother agreed.

Nora laughed and said, "I talked to that Chinese girl on the plane. Her name is Lila. She didn't come from Hong Kong. She came from Formosa, but she was going to Washington, D.C., with her father and mother. They spoke English, just like us, and they were very nice to us."

"Well, poor little Ah Ping doesn't have any father or mother to be nice to her," said Betsy. "She needs foster parents. That's what the magazine said, foster parents."

Betsy's mother picked up a magazine from a table, and said, "I think you misunderstood what you read in the magazine." She turned the pages quickly. In a few moments she opened the magazine to a picture of a little child. She read everything that was printed beside the picture. Then she said, "You see, Betsy, this advertisement is not asking the foster parents to bring the child to live with them here in the United States. It is asking people to give money for the care of the child in his own country."

"Oh!" said Betsy. "Do you mean that if you and Father sent some money, you would be Ah Ping's foster parents?"

"That's right," her mother replied.

"Then would Star and I be her foster sisters?" asked Betsy.

"I suppose so," her mother answered.

Suddenly Nora said, "Oh, wouldn't it be grand, if we could all be her fosters? How much does it cost?"

Betsy's mother turned to the magazine again. "It costs fifteen dollars a month. That is one hundred and eighty dollars a year," she said.

"I don't know how much that is in Irish money," said Nora. "It sounds like a lot."

"Maybe if we put on a play or something like that, we could make enough money to be fosters," said Betsy.

"What a jolly idea!" Nora exclaimed. "My brothers and sisters and I can do the Irish jigs and all the Irish dances. Do you think anyone would be wanting to pay money to see us dance?"

"Of course, they would, Nora!" Betsy's mother exclaimed. "The idea is wonderful!"

"Oh, Nora! You're a smart one!" Betsy cried. Then she turned to her mother, and said, "Where could we have the performance?"

"I think we could give it in the auditorium of the Community Center," Mother replied.

When Star and Bridget sat down to breakfast, Betsy told them all about Ah Ping and the plan to make some money to send to Hong Kong.

Suddenly Betsy's mother said, "I have an idea. It will soon be Halloween! We could sell tickets for a big Halloween party at the Community Center, and the entertainment would be the Irish dancers."

"Mother!" Betsy cried. "That's better yet!

Then everyone will come in a Halloween costume."

"What would we have to eat?" Star asked. "We have to have refreshments for a party."

Her mother laughed. "Of course, Star! We must have refreshments."

"Would doughnuts and cider be enough?" Betsy suggested.

"I believe so," her mother replied.

"Halloween!" Nora exclaimed. "That's the night the witches ride on their broomsticks."

"And the pucas play in the peat bogs," said Bridget.

"Oh, it's a great night!" said Nora.

"I can't wait to tell everybody at school," said Betsy. "I know they'll all want to come to the party."

What Betsy said was true. Everyone wanted to come to the Halloween party. Even Billy was enthusiastic about raising the money to send to

Ah Ping. "My father is an artist," said Billy. "He'll make some signs to put in store windows. I'm sure he will."

Billy's father did make the signs, and he saw that they were placed in the windows. Betsy's father had the tickets printed, and they sold so fast he had to have more printed. They cost fifty cents apiece.

As Halloween drew near the masks and false faces that were in the shops were bought up quickly, but no one would tell what kind of costume he was planning to wear to the party. Everyone wanted to surprise everyone else. "You'll all know the Kilpatrick children," said Nora. "We'll be in our Irish costumes."

Several days later, when the four girls were walking to school, Nora said, "What will you be wearing on Halloween, Betsy?"

"Oh, that's a secret," Betsy answered.

"You'll tell me, won't you?" asked Star. " 'Cause I'm your sister."

"Maybe, but not now," Betsy answered.

"Well, we have a secret, too," said Nora. "Haven't we, Bridget?"

"Oh, yes!" Bridget answered. "A great big secret."

"Is it about the Halloween party?" said Betsy.

"No use your teasing," Nora replied. "We're not telling, are we, Bridget?"

"Oh, no!" Bridget said. "We could never tell."

Soon the girls reached the corner where Mr. Kilpatrick was directing the traffic. When he saw them, he called out, "Good morning to my little colleens."

"Good morning, Uncle!" said Nora and Bridget.

"Good morning, Mr. Kilpatrick," said Betsy and Star.

"Uncle," said Nora, "have you heard about the Halloween party?"

"And will you be going?" asked Bridget.

"Sure, I know all about it," Mr. Kilpatrick answered. "I've got my costume all ready."

"And will Aunt be going?" asked Nora.

"You don't think your aunt would miss such a party, do you? With the six of you dancing the Irish jigs?" Mr. Kilpatrick replied.

"I'm glad we have our dancing clothes with us," said Nora.

"Betsy won't tell what she's going to wear to the Halloween party," said Star.

"I suppose it's a big secret," said Mr. Kilpatrick.

Betsy laughed. "Oh, yes," she said, "but I'll whisper it to you, Mr. Kilpatrick." The big policeman leaned over, and Betsy whispered in his ear, "I'm going to be you!"

Mr. Kilpatrick was so surprised that he almost called out, "Me!" Instead, he said, "Oh, my! What a surprise that will be!" Then he leaned over again and whispered in Betsy's ear, "Now

I'll tell you a secret. I know someone else who's going to be a policeman."

"Who?" Betsy asked.

"Ah! It's a secret," said Mr. Kilpatrick with a sly smile. Still smiling he blew his whistle, and the cars and busses stopped. The children followed Mr. Kilpatrick across the street. When they reached the other side, they waved good-bye to him and ran on to school.

Betsy could not keep her secret from Star for very many days. Star soon learned that Betsy was going to the Halloween party dressed like a policeman. "I want to be one, too!" said Star.

"All right!" said Betsy. "We'll both be policemen. I didn't think anyone else would think of the costume, but Mr. Kilpatrick said he knows someone else who is going to be a policeman."

"Maybe it's Linda," said Star.

"No!" Betsy replied. "Billy Porter is probably the one."

Betsy's mother sewed up dark blue jackets for Betsy and Star. She put brass buttons on the jackets and made them each a policeman's cap with a shiny black visor. With their hair tucked under their caps and with their dark blue snow pants and black boots, their policemen's uniforms were complete. When Star put on a false face with round pink cheeks, Betsy said Star looked like the policeman for the Seven Dwarfs. Star and Betsy laughed at each other, but when they heard Nora and Bridget coming they quickly hid their costumes.

On October thirty-first all of the children in the school were so busy thinking of Halloween that they all seemed to forget that November first was the last day Mr. Kilpatrick would take them across the street. Even Betsy did not remember.

Meanwhile, Nora and Cormac rehearsed the younger children in the Irish jigs and reels. They danced for their aunt and uncle, and Mr. and

Mrs. Kilpatrick said that they had never seen the Irish dances done so well. Nora whispered to Cormac, "That's blarney! But it's nice."

That evening when Nora and Bridget saw Betsy and Star dressed like policemen they laughed very hard. "Oh, wait until Aunt sees you!" Bridget cried, and she laughed again.

"But wait until they see Aunt!" cried Nora. Bridget and Nora leaned against each other, laughing. Then they giggled as they rode with Betsy and Star all the way to the Community House. Betsy's father and mother arrived early with the four girls. They watched as boys and girls and many fathers and mothers crowded through the doors of the auditorium. All of the children sat down on the floor, but there were chairs in the back of the room for the parents.

Betsy thought she had never seen so many different costumes. There were all kinds of animals. There were cats and rabbits and wolves and donkeys. There were mice and monkeys.

There were pirates and tramps and an organ
grinder. There was a Spanish dancer and several
ballet dancers. There seemed to be someone from
every country in the world as well as ghosts and
hobgoblins. Betsy kept watching for another
policeman. She was sure Billy Porter would be
the one. As more and more children arrived
Betsy failed to see another child dressed as a
policeman. Betsy could not pick out anyone she
knew other than the Kilpatrick children. The
girls were all wearing green skirts and white
blouses. They had little red shawls around their
shoulders, long white stockings, and black
slippers. Cormac and Brian were wearing green
trousers and white shirts. Their high green socks
left their knees bare.

The Irish children were all standing in a
group at the side of the room. With them was a
very large woman in a big flowered dress and a
floppy hat covered with bright paper flowers.
Then Betsy saw another person standing with

the group. He was short and dumpy and dressed like a policeman in a blue coat with brass buttons, blue trousers, snow boots, a cap with a shiny black visor, and clean white gloves such as Mr. Kilpatrick wore when he held up the traffic.

Betsy stared across the room at the plump policeman. Who could he be! Suddenly she knew. Of course, she knew! This policeman was Mrs. Kilpatrick! And the big lady in the flowered dress was Mr. Kilpatrick!

Betsy laughed and took hold of Star's hand. "Come!" she said. "There's Mrs. Kilpatrick dressed up like a policeman! She can't fool us!" Betsy and Star ran across the room to Mrs. Kilpatrick, and Betsy cried, "I know you, Mrs. Kilpatrick! You look wonderful!"

At this moment Betsy's father stood up and blew a whistle. All of the talking in the room stopped, and Betsy and Star sat down on the floor. "The entertainment is about to begin," Betsy's father said. "The Kilpatrick children will show us some Irish dances. Mr. Jones, our new school janitor, is here to play the fiddle." Everyone clapped.

The Kilpatrick children walked up on the stage and formed a circle. The music started, and the children began to dance. Only their feet and legs moved. Their arms were held stiff and straight at their sides. Betsy thought she had never seen such twinkling feet as the black slippers leaped up and down. The children seemed as light and as swift as hummingbirds, and they went through their many jigs and reels with apparently little effort at all. They knew many Irish dances, and the audience clapped loudly and asked for more and more.

After the dances all the children in the room paraded. Betty Jane had come covered with purple balloons and looking like a huge bunch of grapes. She won the first prize. Bill, who had come as a Jack-in-the-box, got the second prize.

At the end everyone removed his mask or false face, and the cider and doughnuts were passed around. When the party was over, all agreed that it was the best Halloween party they had ever attended.

As Betsy and Star climbed into their father's car with Nora and Bridget, Betsy's father said, "We made $187.50."

"Is that enough to take care of Ah Ping?" Betsy asked her mother.

"Yes, indeed!" her mother replied. "It will be enough to take care of her for a whole year."

Just then Mr. and Mrs. Kilpatrick came up to the car to say good night. Betsy called out, "Oh, Mr. Kilpatrick! You were a great lady." Then, looking at Mrs. Kilpatrick, she said, "Do you know what?"

"What?" said Mrs. Kilpatrick.

"You would make a wonderful lady policeman."

"You don't say so!" Mrs. Kilpatrick replied. Nora and Bridget giggled.

At that moment Billy Porter came running up to Mr. Kilpatrick. He had a basket in his arms. "Mr. Kilpatrick!" he said. "Here's a present for you. Because you're leaving all of us at school, we want you to have something special." Billy held out the basket to Mr. Kilpatrick.

Everyone was silent as Mr. Kilpatrick took the basket. "What is it?" he asked.

"It's a puppy!" said Billy. "A police-dog puppy. It's not just from me. It's from all of us, because we're your friends and you're our friend." Then Billy said to Betsy, "It's from all of us to Mr. Kilpatrick, isn't it, Betsy?"

"Yes," said Betsy. "You were nice to bring it, Billy." Betsy realized then that she had been so busy thinking about the Halloween party that she had forgotten today was Mr. Kilpatrick's last day on the corner. She was glad Billy had remembered. From now on there would be a lady policeman every day to take them across the street.

Mr. Kilpatrick was still saying thank you for the puppy when Betsy's father started the car.

The next morning as Betsy and Star and Nora and Bridget neared the corner where Mr. Kilpatrick had always stood, there was no red car. Betsy had always seen the red car before she had seen Mr. Kilpatrick. The children walked on. Soon Betsy could see a group of children standing on the corner. She saw the lady policeman walking toward the opposite side of the street with some kindergarten children. Betsy saw that the police lady was short and plump. Then she saw her turn around. She was Mrs. Kilpatrick! Mrs. Kilpatrick, in the very uniform she had worn the night before! Mrs. Kilpatrick, holding up the traffic with her white gloves, would be seeing the children across the street!

Nora and Bridget giggled. "We knew she was the new policeman all the time," said Bridget.

"She was our big secret," said Nora. Mrs. Kilpatrick's face was smiling and her eyes were twinkling. "Good morning to you," she said to the children.

"Hello, Mrs. Kilpatrick!" said Betsy. "You look simply wonderful!"

"Get along with you," said Mrs. Kilpatrick, "and none of your blarney!"

About the Author

Carolyn Haywood is distinguished both as au-
thor and illustrator of children's books. Her first
story *"B" Is for Betsy* was published in 1939.
Since then she has had twenty-seven others published and has become one of the most widely
read American writers for younger children.

Miss Haywood was born in Philadelphia and

still lives in that city. She is a graduate of the Philadelphia Normal School and studied at the Pennsylvania Academy of Fine Arts, where she was awarded a Cresson European Scholarship for distinguished work.

The models for the illustrations in Miss Haywood's books are the neighborhood children who come to her studio and pose for the drawings. She is also a familiar figure in some of the local schools, where she sketches the children during their recess and lunch periods. A portrait painter, Miss Haywood has specialized in portraits of children. Her experience in this field has given her a sympathetic understanding of children and their interests, which has made her peculiarly well fitted to write and illustrate for them.